A Home for Christmas

Jennifer Conner

EXCERPT FROM A HOME FOR CHRISTMAS

"I'm a problem solver, remember. But, I do have another problem, and I'm not sure what the right answer is. I've wanted to kiss you since the first night I saw you again at the bar."

Her heart sped up. "What's stopping you?"

"Right now…I don't know. I feel that you're afraid to take a chance with another man. But, I'd like to think that I'm not the men from your past."

"I see that with everything you do. You're the problem-solver…what do you want to do?" she asked barely above a whisper.

Editon enfolded her within his arms, and she met his gaze. He took her face in a soft caress, but there was a hint of hesitation. She moved to him, erasing the hesitation in both their minds to draw his face to hers. Kady quivered at the sweet tenderness of his kiss as their lips touched.

ISBN-13:978-1537757537

ISBN-10:1537757539

Chapter One

Kady inched her car through the snow. Her tires left what seemed to be the only tracks in the fresh powder. This fall, the snow came early to Eastern Washington. The quiet town was nestled in darkness, and the vacant streets were cast in an eerie glow. Not a soul was out.

"This is the 'main street'?" Noah asked. "You have got to be kidding me."

"You've been to Vine Grove before to visit Grandma and Grandpa. You don't remember?" Kady tightened her grip on the steering wheel as the car's back tires slipped to the right a few inches.

"That was five years ago, I was eight-years-old. Things seemed…bigger...and *more* then."

"Looks about the same to me."

"I guess it's been the same for the last hundred years around here," Noah mumbled, as he picked up his cell phone again. He'd been glued to the glowing screen of his cell phone since they left California. Normally, Kady would have complained about Noah screen time, but it was a long drive. Kady wanted to say, *you're one of the main reasons we're here*, but she didn't have the energy level for one more fight to rehash things.

"You sure Grams and Grandpa are up this late?" Noah asked.

"I called your Grandma at the last rest stop. She said that it didn't matter what time we got in, and that she would have dinner waiting for us."

"Well, that's one good thing about this day." Noah pulled the hood of his sweat jacket up and slumped down in the seat. "I'm starving."

Kady drove out of town and then turned down the gravel road. Even in the ice and snow, the road was as familiar to her as an old sweater. Memories of walking home from school and throwing rocks into mud puddles flooded back as she drove down the narrow lane.

She inched the car up alongside the house and turned off the ignition. The back door opened, and her mom and dad came out.

"Sweetie!" Her dad grabbed her in a bear hug that practically lifted her off the floor.

"Look at you, Noah. My goodness, you are as tall as your mother." Kady's mom admired her grandson before giving him a hug. "You must have grown two feet since we last saw you."

"Hi, Grandma."

"We can't stand out here in the driveway and freeze. I made a pot roast that is still in the crockpot. Let's get some dinner in both of you before we get settled." Vivian turned on her heels and headed into the house.

As Kady walked in the house, again, memories of her

childhood flooded back. Just like the town, not much had changed. New drapes here, a few new throw pillow there, and a new bookcase.

The four of them ate and carried on a light conversation about the drive up. Kady's mom and dad probably sensed that now was not the time to talk about what had happened over the last six months.

Kady helped her mom wash the dishes, as Noah and her dad carried in a few suitcases from the car.

"Don't worry about the rest of the stuff in the U-Haul, Dad. There is nothing in there that can't wait until tomorrow." Kady wiped her hands on a kitchen towel, and then she went to help. She lugged her suitcase up the narrow stairs and dropped the case to stand in the corner of her old bedroom. Stuffed animals lined the top shelf, and the pictures of her favorite movie stars and bands from high school were still on the wall. She was thirty-one. If she had to live with her mom and dad, she was going to have to update her room. She'd worry about this later. As Kady came back down the stairs, each step she took felt heavy and slow with the world pressing down on her shoulders.

Noah had already pulled out the sleeper sofa and was lying on top of it.

"Let's put some sheets on your bed."

"It's okay." His back was still turned to her. "I'll be fine."

Kady sat on the edge of the mattress which squeaked from her weight. She cringed at the bumpiness and springs pushing through the top. Noah hadn't complained. He was very quiet which was even scarier.

She brushed a chunk of Noah's hair over his ear. Some days he already seemed like a young man and other days he looked like what he was, still a boy. His hair was turning to a sandy brown, just like hers. She leaned over, wrapped her arms around him, and pressed her face to his back.

"Things will get better soon." Kady tried not to let the

tears slip out that she felt hanging on the edges of her lashes.

Noah rolled toward her. His eyes were dark and troubled in the dim light. "You promise?"

"Yeah…" She fought to keep her voice steady. "Yeah…I promise. Things will get better," she repeated.

She and Noah silently lay there in the dark listening to the sounds of her mom and dad bumping around upstairs as they headed for bed. There was nothing more to say to Noah, and she hoped what she'd just said wasn't a lie.

I doubt things could get much worse.

Chapter Two

Kady unpacked what she could—at least what was left of their lives—from the back of the U-Haul. The house felt claustrophobic. Four people in barely over a thousand square feet made it clear as to what it was, a small house. She'd filled up her room with as many boxes as she could and still walk around in the little Habittrail she'd created.

Her room now smelled like smoke from the boxes they'd brought in. Kady needed to get out for a few minutes to clear her head and her nose.

"I'm going to the market to pick up a few things. Is there anything I can get you guys? Kady asked as she grabbed her coat and purse.

"Buy some pop, there's no pop in the house," Noah called out from the sofa.

"Don't buy him soda, it's bad for him," her mom

11

yelled back.

She mouthed, 'okay' to Noah, and he grinned. It was nice to see him smile.

Kady drove the short distance back into town. She steered her car into one of the nearly vacant parking slots at Rays Cash and Carry Mart. She sat watching the snow fall on the windshield and be wiped away, to gather her thoughts. Kady dashed into the store and then put the groceries in the trunk.

Back in the car, she drummed her fingers on the steering wheel and looked at the clock on the dashboard. It was still early, they wouldn't miss her for a few minutes.

The neon red and blue lights of *The Steer In* blinked, beckoning her in the darkness. Kady scooped up her purse and headed across the two-lane main street.

She opened the door and was assaulted with loud jukebox music mixed with the smell of peanuts and the acidic fragrance of hops from beer. She walked up to the bar and took a seat. After a moment, the bartender came toward her.

"What can I get you?"

She opened her wallet and looked at the five and two ones nestled there. Just one drink, she could afford that. "Do you have cherry rum?" she asked.

"Nope," the bartender answered wiping his hands on a towel. "But, we have rum and we have cherries, would that do?"

"Sure."

A man slid onto the bar stool next to her. "Fancy seeing you in a place like this."

The oldest line in the book. Kady rolled her eyes and faced the man. "Listen, buddy, you are trying to pick up the *wrong* girl tonight. A man is the *last* thing I need right now. I need a job. I need money. I need a life. Unless you can supply me with any of those things, then beat it."

Instead of being offended, the man laughed.

"I didn't mean what I said as a joke," she said curtly.

"Kady, it's me, Editon. Man, I must look different because I know that we're both older, but I recognized you right away." He smiled making little-crinkled lines form in the corners of his eyes.

"Editon? Editon Rain?" She looked closer. She did recognize him. The dark brown eyes and his part-Native American jet black hair brought back recognition.

"My God, it's been…what?" He stopped in thought.

"Thirteen years since our senior year in high-school." The bartender set down the rum with a small cup of cherries in front of her. "Let's toast to old times." Kady grabbed the shot glass and downed the rum.

"Okay…" Editon watched her. "Can I buy you another?"

"Sure," she said, as she let the rum trail in spiral paths to warm her insides.

He motioned to the bartender, who brought the bottle and filled her glass.

"Hanging out at the bar. I guess that's what people still do for excitement around here?"

"I wouldn't know." He shrugged a broad shoulder. "Not really."

"*You're* hanging out here. What are you drinking? I should offer to buy *you* a drink."

Those dark brown intense eyes were still watching her. She had to break eye contact and finally look down. It was like he was trying to figure her out.

"You can if you want, but it's just ginger ale and lime." He swirled the contents of his glass. "I don't drink. I'm here because that's my brother, Nahko." He motioned to the bartender who waved a hand before going back to talk with a patron. "You probably don't remember him from school, he's a few years older. Anyway, I promised I'd hang around the bar cleared out and help him with a broken pipe under the sink."

"You're a plumber?"

"I'm kind of a jack-of-all-trades. Call me a handy man. I help where I can." He leaned an arm on the bar and Kady noticed the Native American tattoos that wound around his bicep. "I heard you were back in town."

"Yep…so you probably also know that I'm living with my mom and dad."

"I lived with my mom and dad for a few years until I got some money."

She drank her second shot, and Editon's brother filled up her glass again. She downed that too. The light feeling of a buzz closed in and clouded her mind. They sat and listened to the music.

She tried not to think about the rest of her life and enjoy the moment she had.

"Well, it seems that you want to drink in peace. I'll leave you alone. Let me know when you want to cash out, and I will pay Nahko."

"You said you would buy me *one* drink."

"Don't worry about it. I'll take care of it," Editon said, as he slipped off the bar stool to shoot a round of pool.

Kady sat and listened to the music on the jukebox. One country song. One eighties rock song. And then back to country. She lost track of time. It was nice for a change.

When she looked up, she had been there for nearly two hours. Shaking her head, she smiled at Editon and started to stand.

"You ready to go?" he asked.

"Yes…" She grabbed the edge of the bar. "Whoa…" she said, surprised by the spinning room.

Editon was there with his hand on her elbow to steady her. "I'm going to drive you home."

"I'm…" she started to say 'fine' but knew that she wasn't. "Thanks. I'd appreciate it."

When they got outside, she motioned across the street.

"What about my car?"

"Don't worry about it. We'll get it tomorrow."

He helped her to the parking lot and unlocked his pickup. It was new, shiny, and expensive.

"I only ask one thing," he requested. "You can't throw up in my rig, I've only had it a month."

"I promise I won't," she said, embarrassed. She slid in the front seat.

Editon got in and said, "Put on your seatbelt. The roads are still icy."

She clicked closed the buckle. As he pulled out, Kady's head swam more. *How much did I drink?*

The night and the darkness seemed to envelop her. Her head slumped over and landed on Editon's shoulder. He felt solid, the first solid thing in her fluid world that she'd felt in months. She inhaled. He smelled like firewood and cedar trees. The brush of leather from his coat was cool against her cheek.

I'll just close my eyes for…

"Kady?" A deep voice pulled her awake from the nice dream she was having. Editon straightened her in the car seat. "Are you okay?" he asked, concern etching his brow.

She rubbed at her eyes. "Yeah…I'm fine."

"We're here."

"Where?" she asked, disoriented.

"Your mom and dad's house. I remembered where they lived. When you live in Vine Grove, you pretty much know where everyone lives." He reached across her and unhooked her seatbelt. "You gonna be okay?" he asked again.

"Yep." Kady shook her head to clear it and rubbed a hand over her face. She looked at his leather coat and felt her cheeks heat. "Here I was accusing you of trying to pick me up at the bar, and I'm the one who slobbered all over you in the car."

"I think you were asleep. Short nap. That doesn't really count." His smile was easy, and it lit his eyes.

She slid her legs out and stood. "Thanks for making sure I got home safe."

"You're welcome. And, when it comes down to who's picking up who, I'm the one who got to take you home at the end of the night." He winked, making something flutter in the pit of her stomach.

Kady took a pen out of her purse and reached for his hand. "Here's my number, why don't you call me." She inched up his sleeve and wrote her cell on his wrist."

He smiled and pulled the sleeve back over his wrist. "I'll see you around, Kady Randall."

The only light still on in the house was over the sink in the kitchen. Her parents went to bed early. Her dad's motto was always, *early to bed, early to rise*. Farmers were like that year-round, not just during the growing season. This was a good thing, she'd hate to face them.

Kady slipped her coat off her shoulders, took off her boots and set them by the front door.

She got about half-way across the living room.

"I thought you were going out for a few groceries, not to get drunk and pick up guys." The computer screen lit the glare on Noah's face.

"I didn't…well, I did have a few drinks, but I hadn't really planned to. Editon was buying."

"At least the two of you are on a first name basis."

"We knew each other from school."

"That makes it better? And…you forgot the pop."

"It's back in our car… which is back at the store. Sorry." Kady sighed. "I can't have this conversation right now. I'm going to bed. I'll see you in the morning." She started to turn away and then stopped, remembering her rule of never going to bed angry. "I love you."

"Yeah…" Noah muttered as he flipped his computer

closed and tossed it over on the other side of the bed.

Chapter Three

Kady woke to the rumble of a truck outside. She sat up in bed and the vice of her hangover wound down on her head. "Ow." She pressed her hands against her temples and reached for the glass of water on the nightstand.

She stood and then tiptoed across the cold, creaky wood floor to peek out the window. Why did a wood floor feel so much colder in the winter?

Editon and Nahko were outside talking with her dad. They'd brought her car back. She remembered that Editon drove her home and that she'd left her car at the store. He'd offered the take her home because she'd had enough liquor in her to light a tiki torch. She'd been friends with Editon in high school, and he obviously was still a nice guy.

When her eyes could focus again, she would go and

thank him in person…just not now.

****

There was a knock on the door of Editon's shop. When he opened it, he was surprised to see Kady standing on the porch.

"Hey." He brushed off his hands and moved to the side to let her in. "What are you doing here?"

"I wanted to thank you and your brother for bringing back my car." She looked down at her feet when she spoke. "I had no plans to drink last night. I never do…but I guess I did."

"No problem. I didn't want your car sitting in the lot."

"How did you get it back without the keys?"

"When I stopped by this morning to buy juice at Ray's, I peeked in your car's window and the keys were still in the ignition." He grinned. "I'm not a very good carjacker."

Her eyes widened for a second and then she blushed.

"I guess that shows you what kind of state of mind I was in last night."

"That good, huh?"

"How did you know where I lived?"

"You said you'd moved in with your parents. I remembered their house when we rode the school bus together."

She looked around. "Is this where you live?"

"No." He was surprised she would think that. "It's my shop. I use it for the projects I'm working on." Editon looked at the way the light came through the window and caught the gold in her blonde hair. It tumbled out the sides of her furry winter hat. In high-school, Kady was pretty, but now, she was definitely a beautiful woman. He'd had such a crush on her, but thirty-year-olds didn't have crushes.

"Can I take you out for a late breakfast to thank you for driving me home?" she asked.

"You don't need to…"

She smiled. "I'd like to. That is, if you aren't too busy."

"Sure." He didn't want to sound too anxious. "Let me put a few things away and get my keys." He hurried into his office and spotted the clean shirt he'd hung on a hook. *Thank goodness.* The one he was wearing smelled like a sweaty oil can. He'd just taken a shower so hopefully, he still smelled better than the shirt. He quickly stuck his arms through the sleeves and buttoned the fresh garment.

Editon locked the front door on the way out, and then said, "Let's go."

He picked Bean and Dreams café guessing that at this time of the morning they might not be too busy. His hunch paid off. There were only a few tables filled in the café. They each ordered coffee and then biscuits and gravy.

Editon slid an arm along the wood booth and leaned

back. "Even though it's been so many years, it felt like it was yesterday when I saw you walk into the bar last night."

Kady looked out the window. A distant smile curved her lips. "Only yesterday plus a dozen and a million years."

"You disappeared from school like a puff of smoke. Did you decide not to graduate?"

"I had every intention and then on to college, but life intervened. I guess you hadn't heard. I became pregnant with Noah." As the waitress poured coffee into her cup, Kady added a splash of creamer.

"I never knew. One day you were there and the next day you were gone. Why didn't you stay in school? It wasn't the 1950s."

"My dad's a great dad. The best in the world. But he's old-fashioned. When Tad Walton offered to take me away—"

"Tad Walton was the father?"

"Yeah…I've never had great luck picking men.

Anyway, Tad offered to take me to California and move in with his aunt. After we settled in I was eight-months pregnant and he hooked up with an older woman. She told him that she could help his acting career."

"Did she?"

"No. He was in a few ads in the local newspaper for a burger joint, but he always thought it would lead to the big screen. That was when he left, and I had to move out of the aunt's house. I haven't seen or heard from his since." Kady took a drink of her coffee and then stirred it again with her spoon.

"He left you and his baby? When you were eight months pregnant?" Even though there was nothing he could do about the past now, anger churned through Editon, "I never liked that guy. How could he do that to you?"

"We were eighteen. I thought he loved me."

"You could have come back."

"No, I couldn't really. I got a job and my GED. When

Noah was born, he became my life. I wanted to prove to myself and to Noah that we could make it on our own."

"And you did?"

"Noah and I did. It wasn't easy, but we did."

Editon thanked the waiter and cut into his biscuits and gravy. "How is it?" he asked.

"I forgot about Meg's biscuits and gravy." She sighed and closed her eyes. "They really are the best in the world."

Editon chuckled. "They are pretty darn great, aren't they?" He took another bite, chewed, and swallowed before speaking again. "At the bar last night you said that you needed a job?"

"I finished my college degree to be a teacher, and I did my student teaching in California. I had checked before we moved back here if there were openings at Vine Grove Elementary, but there are no positions open right now. I'm not sure now what I am going to do. Start over from scratch once again probably. I'm living with my mom and dad. I doubt they will kick us out."

"Are you planning on staying in Vine Grove? Why don't you move somewhere where there are openings for teachers?" he asked.

"We can't right now. Noah and I literally have what I fit in the U-Haul when we left a few days ago."

"If you don't mind me asking, what happened in California? Why didn't you stay?"

"I don't want rumors to spread." Kady looked nervously around the restaurant. "Noah needs a fresh start, that's one of the reasons we came back...well that, and we had to." She bit her lip. Her gaze met his, and there were questions in her eyes. He could see that she wanted to have faith in him. "Promise you won't spread this around town. Noah needs to get settled."

"You can trust me. I'm not one of the gossips from the Grange Hall." Editon took Kady's hand and gave it a squeeze. "You can trust me," he repeated.

"Thanks. I really appreciate it." Kady took a shaky breath and looked as though she was going to cry. He squeezed her hand again.

"What happened?"

"Noah's a really good kid. Smart. He's in advanced classes in middle school. He loves math and wants to go into the field. In California, the only place we could afford to live was a mobile home park outside of Hayward. I was gone, finishing up my classes, and he was bored. Noah started hanging out with some kids from the park. They wanted him to start committing crimes. Petty stuff. Stealing purses out of unlocked cars, taking kids bicycles and reselling them."

"Did he get arrested?" Editon asked.

"He was never arrested but did go along as the lookout a few times. He thought they were fun to hang around with at first, but when they started to get deeper into crime and wanted to steal cars and rob people in the park, he said no."

"I take it his answer didn't go over well."

Kady's laugh was stiff. "That is an understatement. One night a bullet shattered his bedroom window. The bullet hit the wall a foot above his head. That was when I knew that we had to move."

"Are you sure it was these kids?"

"Yes. Noah saw them drive away. That was when Noah told me about what was happening."

"This made up your mind?"

"I called around to find a new place to live and we were going to move in a few days. A few nights later, I had a final at school when the same boys from the park launched fireworks into the side of the mobile home. It's dry. It's California. The grass along one side ignited. The whole mobile home went up in flames in a matter of minutes. Noah was inside." A shudder passed through her.

"Was he hurt?" Editon watched the fear in Kady's eyes as she relived the memories.

"His hands received minor burns. He stayed inside and

tried to collect up as many things as he could and threw them out the door. Noah saved things you wouldn't think a thirteen-year-old would save, like our photo album. The fire department arrived quickly, but most everything went up in the fire. I was so scared when I got the call, a girlfriend had to drive me home. Noah just should have gotten out...he could have died."

"But he didn't. He's fine."

"He felt..." she paused and then added, "He *feels* so guilty for what happened. He's a good kid."

"I can only imagine how difficult it is to move back here to your mom and dad's house. But things will get better."

"That's what I told Noah last night. I hope I can believe it."

"No fire insurance?"

"Nothing to cover as much damage as we received. I had the minimal coverage that I could afford which I found out was next to nothing."

Editon leaned back and pushed his plate off to the side. "There are a few advantages to being in a small town. You hear things good and bad. I happen to know that a shop in town, Que Syrah Syrah, is looking for help."

"I'm not familiar with it."

"It only opened in the past year. It's a cute little wine shop. About six months ago, the owner, Tegan, married August who runs a vineyard. I had dinner with them last week, and she told me that she wants to take more time off, but hasn't had any luck finding anyone she trusts with the shop."

"Thanks for thinking of me. It sounds like a good opportunity."

"I know it's not perfect, but, you told me that there are no teacher openings right now. Tegan's super sweet and I think she would be easy to work for. If you are interested, I can pass on your number."

"Let me find a piece of paper and I'll write it down." Kady fumbled in her purse.

Editon grinned. "Don't worry. I already have it." He inched up his sleeve to expose the number she'd written on his wrist the night before.

Kady's cheeks turned to an adorable shade of deep pink. She rolled her eyes. "I guess some things don't change from school. How junior high can I be?"

"I'll never take a shower or wash my arm again." Editon faked a swoon and put his hand over his heart. His comment made her laugh, and her eyes brightened. Editon wanted to keep her happy, he didn't like it when she was unhappy. He picked the bill off the table.

"Hey." Kady reached for it. "I said that I would buy."

He maneuvered it out of her grasp. "Don't worry about it. Spending time with you again was thanks enough." He paused, as he took out his wallet and tossed down a twenty-dollar bill. "Do you need me to drive you somewhere?"

"No. Thanks. I'll walk."

"I'll stop by Tegan's shop and give her your number." He slid out of the booth and stood. "Maybe I can see you again?"

She smiled up at him, and his biscuits and gravy did a little flip in his stomach. "When I get settled. I'd like that. Maybe in a week or two?"

He was hoping Kady was going to say tomorrow, but he was a patient man.

"Sure. In a week or two. I'll see you soon."

Chapter Four

Kady took the job at Que Syrah Syrah, and life was starting to feel like it was finally falling into place once again one small piece at a time. Just as Editon assured her, Tegan was easy to work for, and she and Kady became fast friends. It had been a long time since Kady felt she had 'girlfriends.' When she was alone in California, she was always so busy that she barely had time to eat and sleep.

The rustic shop was filled with wine racks and cute rustic knick-knacks. Tegan had good taste and displayed the items to draw interest. She also encouraged local groups to meet at the shop.

A couple times a month, this particular group of women met at the wine shop. Tegan told her that it had started out to be a 'book club' but they admitted that they were really there to chat and drink some of Tegan's new wines. Tonight was one of the ladies meeting nights.

Kady dusted off the shelves, as the women talked and laughed.

"We can laugh about this all we want, but we've had a pretty good track record so far with The Love List. A lot of the people we have paired up have stuck." Tegan tipped her glass forward to make a point.

"You didn't get August when you drew out a name," Chloe pointed out.

"No, I drew Richard."

"Who tried to burn down your shop?"

"Yes…but, because of going out to the Vineyard to meet Richard, the psycho, I met August the wonderful." Tegan grinned.

"It's kind of like the degrees of Kevin Bacon game?" Rebecca said.

"You end up with who you should be with. Our

random drawing is just that, random. But, it might help you think of someone in town you never expected," Tegan said, as she turned and shook the basket in Kady's direction. "Ready to jump back into the dating game and give The Love List a try?"

Kady looked around the circle of women. "I'm happy this 'Love List' has worked out for most of you...but, I think I'll pass. I don't have room for Mr. Right."

"Everyone has room for 'Mr. Right'. " Tegan said with a laugh.

"Well, not me." Kady went back to dusting the shelves.

"Maybe next time." Tegan shook the basket once more and placed it back on the table.

The bell sounded over the front door, and Kady looked up. She was surprised when Editon walked through. Kady ran a hand through her loose hair which had slipped from her ponytail. Of course, she wore her baggier jeans and a stained

T-shirt.

"Editon." Tegan jumped up and went to give him a hug. "How are you?"

"I'm fine." He held a single white lily in his hand.

"Can I help you with something? Do you have a date?" Tegan asked as she looked at the flower.

"Not exactly." He shook his head. "I'm here to see Kady."

"Kady?" Tegan looked from Editon to Kady, and then back. "*Our* Kady?"

"Unless there is another Kady here, I'm talking about the one who is standing behind the counter. I don't mean to jump into your group here. I'd stopped and got this flower…and then I was going to go over to her house, but I saw the lights on and…"

Kady had to admit that Editon was even cuter when he was flustered.

Tegan grinned. "Well, don't just stand there, Editon.

Give Kady the flower."

He walked over and handed her the lily. Kady took it and heard the other women sigh. These women were hopeless romantics, and as much as she tried to deny it, so was she.

Editon took her elbow and led her to the far side of the shop and hopefully out of ears' reach of the others.

He spoke first. "Sorry that I just 'showed up' but I was waiting for you to call. When you didn't…I thought I'd take the proverbial bull by the horns and show up in person. I didn't know that there would be a full house here."

"It's fine. They meet a couple of times a month, and it's informal. It's all my fault. I meant to call a million times, it's just been so hectic learning a new job and then getting settled."

"I didn't want to push things. I know you've been through a lot. Then I thought maybe you didn't want to see me again, but I didn't get that from our last meeting." He picked at an imaginary chip of paint on the counter.

Kady put a hand on his forearm and then looked at the women who were trying not to gawk at them. She pulled her hand back. "No…that's the complete opposite. I did…do, want to see you again."

He let free an audible breath as if he'd been holding it in. "How about tomorrow night? I'm not going to leave it up to chance this time."

"Tegan is gone for a few days and this is the first time I'm covering the shop on my own tomorrow."

"Would you like for me to come over and help?" There was eagerness in the tone of his voice.

"No." Kady shook her head. "I've got it, and I think I have *almost* all the types of wine memorized."

"Why don't you pick out your favorite bottle and I'll pick you up after the shop closes."

"That sounds like fun." She looked down at the lily. "Thanks for the flower. I don't remember the last time that a guy brought me flowers."

"We'll have to remedy that. It's only *one* flower this time, but next time I'll work on a whole bouquet." He grinned as he took her hand and kissed the back of her knuckles.

There was another sigh from the group.

"I'll see you tomorrow." He turned to face the women as he pulled out his white and black knit hat with flaps over the ears. He wiggled it on making tufts of black hair stick out the front. "Evening ladies. Thanks for letting me crash your party for a few minutes."

"Anytime, Editon." When Editon shut the door, and the engine of his truck started, Tegan lifted the wicker basket with the names off the table and rummaged around until she found the scrap of paper she was looking for. "Editon…" she read the name out loud and then continued. "I guess he's out of the single guy pool."

"We just met…well actually, again. We knew each

other from high school," Kady said.

"I saw the way he looked at you," Tegan held her gaze.

"It's not like we are 'seeing' each other. You can leave Editon's name in the basket," Kady said as she slammed the feather duster back on the counter.

"I'm taking his name out for now. Unless you want to choose another name?" Tegan shook the slips in the basket again.

"No. I don't." Kady crossed her arms over her chest.

"I didn't think so. Editon's a great guy." Chloe chimed in. "He's done so much for Vine Grove."

"I'm happy he's a helpful handyman," Kady said. "But, I need a man with a *real* job. Money. I don't know, a life?"

"What has he told you about what he does?" Tegan asked with a raise of her brow.

"Not much…why?" Kady asked.

"You can clear things up tomorrow night," Tegan said as she stood to clear the fruit and cheese plate from the table. "I was under the same misimpression of August the first time I met him. I wouldn't have cared what he did for a living, but let's just say it worked out for the best."

"I'm not ready for a relationship," Kady stated as she grabbed a few empty glasses and placed them in the sink.

"He's just asking you on a date. Give him a chance," Tegan said with the last sip from her wine glass.

"Fine. If it keeps me from drawing from your silly basket of names, then I'll do it."

Chapter Five

The sluggish day moved as fast as molasses in January as more snow fell outside Que Syrah Syrah. With the weather being awful, only one customer came into the shop. Since Tegan had left that morning for a few days out of town, the place seemed extra quiet. After almost nodding off to sleep once, Kady had to turn on the radio to keep herself awake.

She propped her hands under her chin and looked out the window, watching snowflakes drift down and cover the ground in a blanket of white. In a few hours, those inches had piled higher, and Kady began to worry. It was less than six-miles back to her mom and dad's house, but her car had nearly bald tires, and she knew that they would be no good for driving in the snow. The radio predicted six more inches, so it was bound to become worse.

There was a jingle of the bell over the front door making her jump. She spun around to find Editon shaking the snow off his hat and coat like a big dog.

"What are you doing here?" she asked. Kady held her voice steady but in reality, she was relieved to see another human being...especially a six-foot plus hunky one.

"We have a date tonight, right?" He pulled his hat off and wadded it into his hand.

"I figured because of the weather you would call it off. Besides, it's not evening yet."

"The weather is bad out there. There is a lot more snow than they had originally predicted. I wanted to make sure you were all right here at the shop and to tell you the bad news that there's a tree over the main road."

"How am I going to get home?" she asked more to herself than to him.

"It's going to be at least a few hours until it's cleared

and the road reopens." Unzipping his coat, he walked toward her.

Kady bit her lip. "I was just looking around the shop and thinking about a worse case scenario. There are wood benches and a few quilts in the back. I guess I could stay here."

"Why don't you come with me? My house is just about a half-mile from here."

"I can't. The shop is still open for a few more hours, and I can't leave early."

He frowned. "I don't think anyone is coming out in this storm."

"Well, if they do, I need to stay—" Kady was half-way through her sentence when the lights went out. She finished with, "Open. Wow…it's dark in here. And I'm not sure if there are any flashlights." She could barely see Editon who stood a few feet from her a few feet in front of her. Even though it was late afternoon, the storm made it as dark as night. "I don't want to move. I'm afraid I might break something."

He stepped closer. "I have an idea. I remember seeing a table of candles to our right."

"Yes, there is. But those are candles for *sale,* not for power outages."

Slowly, he moved away. In a few moments, a lighter sparked that he held and then he lit two candles. He came back toward Kady and handed her one. He lifted a twenty-dollar bill up and dropped it on the checkout counter. He chuckled. "I'm buying a few right now to get us through this pinch, so don't worry about it."

"You don't need to do that," she protested.

"We can't stumble around here in the dark. I'm a problem-solver."

"I see that." She had to laugh. It was silly to buy fancy scented candles to light the darkness, but what else could they do?

"What was that about keeping the shop open for a few more hours?"

Kady tried to muster up a protest, but the temperature in the small space was already dropping, and she shivered. "You're right again. It would be meaningless to stay open *and* freeze to death. You'll cover for me and make sure that Tegan knows that the power went out?"

"Of course," he answered. Lit by the glow of the candlelight, Editon's handsome features were more pronounced.

"But if the power is out here, won't it be out at your house too?" she asked.

"I have a generator, Que Syrah Syrah does not."

"Okay…you win. *And* you have something warm to drink?" she asked hopefully.

"How does hot chocolate with spray can whip cream and homemade chicken noodle soup sound?"

"It sounds like possibly the best meal in the history of

the world." She grinned, happy that Editon was the one who came to rescue her.

Kady snuggled down into the seat of Editon's pickup and further under the blanket he'd laid over her lap to keep her warm. She rubbed her hands in front of the truck's heater.

She looked out the window and watched the wipers try and keep up with the heavy falling snow. "Can you see?"

"Good thing I know this road like the back of my hand. It would be difficult for someone who didn't to even stay on the road."

"No kidding." Kady gripped the seatbelt a little tighter. "You said you live close by?"

"There's my house." He pointed to a enormous log cabin in the distance as they crept down the driveway.

"That's your house?" She tried to keep the shock out of her voice.

"Sure is. I built it myself." He pulled the truck up to the house and hit the garage opener. Waiting until the door slid open, he inched the truck into the open spot. Then he jumped out, - came around and opened her door. She followed him inside. "I'm going to start a fire. Make yourself at home."

Kady set her purse on the concrete mahogany-stained counter and checked out the large kitchen. A six-burner gas stove with double ovens sat on one side of the room. Expensive copper chef pans hung above the island casting a warm glow off the sheen.

"Do you like to cook?" she asked.

"I do. I'm getting pretty good at it the more I try new things."

"This is the kitchen of my dreams." She turned in a circle taking in the twenty-plus foot ceilings with open wood beams over the living room. Native American art and woven blankets adorned the walls.

She came to stand beside him, as he knelt beside the hearth. "This house is amazing. How many square feet is it?"

"It's about twenty-five hundred upstairs and about the same—maybe a little more—downstairs. The lower level isn't finished yet, getting closer, but not complete. It took me over eight years to build this much. I work on the rest when I can." When the flame ignited in the fireplace, Editon stood and brushed bark off his hands. He looked at her and his brow furrowed. "Is something wrong?"

"Your home isn't at all what I expected. I thought you were a handyman."

"I am, and I told you I was a handy man. I like to build things and always have a project going. I have a few large things that are going to keep me busy for the next few years."

"But, how can you afford a house like this? Vine Grove isn't what you'd call the millionaire capital of the world to have an income for a house like this."

He laughed. "I'm going to make us that hot chocolate, and we can talk more."

After the teapot had whistled Editon poured the hot water into two cups. "Would you like a little Bailey's Irish Cream in yours?" he asked.

"Sure."

He stirred the cups, handed her one and followed her back to the living room. They sat on the floor in front of the fire. Kady laid her cup down and then warmed her hands in front of the flames.

"This was a great idea. My hands were turning into ice at the shop."

He took her hands, rubbed them with his, and then blew a warm breath on her fingers.

"Are you going to tell me how you live in a mansion?" she asked with a chuckle.

"It's not a mansion...I was planning on the house being much smaller, but I was bored, and I kept building.

When I graduated from high school and turned eighteen, I became eligible for my grandmother's tribe's money. She is a part of the Shakopee Mdewakanton Tribe. I guess, fortunately, it's one of the richest tribes in the country. She takes pride in our heritage and even named us. My name means, standing as a sacred object."

"She's not from Washington State?"

"No. My family moved here from Minneapolis. That's where she lives. Anyway, she gets her tribal money which is over a million and a half a year."

Kady's cup stopped halfway to her mouth. "Did you say million?"

He nodded. "Since Nahko and I are fifty percent Shakopee, we get a share too. After high school, I went to visit Grandma for a few months but liked Washington State better. I moved back to Vine Grove to be with Nahko and our parents. A short time later, Mom and Dad were killed in a car accident."

"I'm so sorry." Kady placed a hand on his.

"It seems now like a long time ago. I bounced around here, wasted a lot of time and brain cells. Mainly, I sat around playing video games and smoking dope. Not a time I'm really proud of. I was finally a popular kid in town when I had a perpetual party going on. That was until my grandma showed up on my doorstep. She was not going to have me waste my life *or* our tribe's money. That was not what it was for. She put her foot down and told me she didn't care where, but I was going to college. The tribal money covered a scholarship so I picked Stanford and acquired a master's in business."

"A masters...wow. We were both in California at the same time, and we never saw each other." She shook her head in disbelief.

"I didn't know where you had gone, or I would have looked you up."

"Except that, I was in night classes at a community

college while you were at Stanford."

"All education is good. I was fortunate with the opportunity. After college graduation, I came back to Vine Grove. I studied the stock market and made worthy investments in small start-up companies who are not so small any longer." He laughed. "Grandma also told Nahko and me that she would share her wealth if we would help her make the world a better place. Use this money for good, she told us. This is what we have been trying to do."

"Your brother owns a bar. How does that fit in?"

"Yeah, well that's bending the rules a bit, but it makes him happy. He tries to keep the regulars out of trouble, and he likes being social. He spends the rest of his time helping the community here and around the world as I do."

"Does everyone know about your money?"

"No. Very few." Editon shook his head. "I don't invite many people out to my house…mainly only women who are stranded in snowstorms." He pushed up on his hands and stood. "I'm going to heat up the soup. I'm starving, what about you?"

"I *am* hungry," she admitted. She hadn't thought about it until he mentioned it and now her stomach growled in protest.

Kady sat on a stool at the kitchen counter and watched Editon move easily around the kitchen. He was so different than the other men she'd spent time with. He was laid-back and happy-go-lucky. Such a nice change from the sulky guys with baggage she seemed to end up dating. She and Editon weren't really dating, but this was a date, *right*? Even if it was fueled by a snowstorm and started a few hours early, he'd still asked her out.

He toasted sourdough bread and placed a slice on each plate with a steaming bowl of soup and fresh butter. They went back into the living room and sat again by the fire. Making small talk through dinner, they caught up on each other's life and the parts they'd missed out on over the years.

Editon cleared the plates and put the extra soup away as Kady called home to tell her family what happened.

He put another log on the fire. When he turned, Editon saw her shiver. "I wish it were a little warmer in here. The generator doesn't seem to keep things running at a hundred percent, but the fireplace should start kicking out good heat soon. Come here." He scooted closer and pulled her against him. He whipped a wool blanket off the couch and wrapped it around them. "Nothing works better than body heat." He grinned with adorable boyish charm.

"You mentioned that you would be busy with projects coming up. What are you working on?" Kady let herself be enveloped in his warmth. It seeped into her bones and soothed her.

"Nahko and me—well, mainly me—are building a large community center outside of town. Originally, we were going to build it on tribal land, but we came up against blockades."

"What happened?" she asked.

"Nahko and I decided that it needed to be open to all the people in the community and not just the tribe. This area, except for the wine industry, experiences some pretty severe economic struggles. The local kids need a place to go after school. A safe place. And not just the kids. The elderly and everyone in between."

"That's great...*wow*. Really great. If there had been a place for Noah like that in California, we might not have had these problems."

"That's what we want to see." Editon gave an understanding nod. "Most kids aren't bad, they're bored. When they are bored, they get into trouble. Keep them busy and there are fewer problems."

"True." Kady watched the flames of the fire reflect in the dark of Editon's eyes. "I think that it may not have been so bad that I came home to Vine Grove."

"I'm thinking that too." Editon reached out and ran a

thumb down her cheek. "I've got a terrible confession. I've been debating if I should say anything or not."

"You're married?" Momentary panic gripped her.

"No…" He chuckled. "I haven't been a saint, but I've never found anyone special. The night I saw you at Nahko's bar all my old feelings flooded back. I had such a crush on you in school."

"Really?" Kady was surprised.

"Oh yeah…like a lost puppy. I would follow you around about ten paces behind just to be in the same space as you. A little stalkerish, I know. Back then I didn't know what that was."

Kady took his hand and rubbed the back with her fingers. "Why didn't you ever say anything?"

"You would have never gone out with someone like me. I was a shy geek. You were so pretty…perfect."

"Perfect? Hardly. I didn't know what I wanted at that age. I thought Tad. I wanted Tad…and Tad was a loser."

"He gave you Noah."

"You're right. The only good thing Tad ever did. I wonder how different my life would have been if I'd stayed in Vine Grove and had Noah?" Kady wondered.

"What ifs are the bane of our existence aren't they? I try and let things go. Look ahead and turn the what-ifs into a future question."

"You have a point."

"I'm a problem solver, remember. But, I do have another problem, and I'm not sure what the right answer is. I've wanted to kiss you since the first night I saw you again at the bar."

Her heart sped up. "What's stopping you?"

"Right now...I don't know. I feel that you're afraid to take a chance with another man. But, I'd like to think that I'm not the men from your past."

"I see that with everything you do. You're the problem-solver...what do you want to do?" she asked barely above a whisper.

Editon enfolded her within his arms, and she met his gaze. He took her face in a soft caress, but there was a hint of hesitation. She moved to him, erasing the hesitation in both their minds to draw his face to hers. Kady quivered at the sweet tenderness of his kiss as their lips touched.

He put his hands on her arms and ran them in a sensuous slide up and down until she forgot that she didn't need another man in her life. Editon deepened the kiss until she forgot to breathe. His breath was uneven as his warm, and his solid body engulfed her.

Editon finally sat back. "*Damn*. Just damn." His eyes were a little dazed. "I'd dreamed kissing you would be good, but in reality, it's much better."

It had been a long time since a man looked at her like Editon did at this moment. Kady wasn't finished yet. She wanted more.

She wrapped her arms around his neck and pulled him

to her again. She kissed him until they finally had to break apart to breathe.

Editon brushed his hand over his mouth. "I'm a problem-solver and what my solving abilities are telling me is not very gentlemanly." He grinned a sensual smile that sent a skitter of sexual tension through her spine. "We're going to stop here...for now. If I don't, I'm not sure how much willpower I have. I don't want to, but I'm going to leave now and see if the road is open. I'll be back."

When the front door clicked closed, Kady hugged her arms around her middle. She liked Editon. She liked Editon a lot! She hadn't planned on that...but, she hadn't planned on many things that happened in her life. Why not leave space for *unexpected good* things? Kady thought of the Love List drawing, happy now that she hadn't taken a name because right now the only man she wanted was Editon.

Editon was back in a half-hour. He shook his head as he took off his coat and hat and hung them on a hook by the door. "The road's still closed. Now there are power lines down, and the trucks are working on them. It's a big old mess. I asked them when they thought it would be open, and they had no idea."

"Huh…what should I do?"

"I think it's a no-brainer. You have to stay. It's the safest option. Noah is fine with your mom and dad."

"I guess you're stuck with me." She couldn't argue. It was the best solution.

"Things could be worse." He grinned. "Now it's *your* turn to warm up *my* hands." He came to her, and she rubbed his hands like he'd done to hers. "Since you're stuck, you're spending the night, but you're going to sleep in the spare bedroom. This is really our first date, and I want a second."

"I'd like that too."

"I'm going to make some popcorn, and I'll let you pick out a movie. The DVD's are in a cabinet next to the TV."

They snuggled on the couch, watched a silly comedy and laughed until her sides hurt. It felt good to laugh, it had been too long since she had. Editon loaned her a pair of shorts and a T-shirt, and they soaked in the hot tub on his deck, drank more hot chocolate, and watched the snowfall around them. She could see the outline of the valley below and bet the view was a knock-out when it was clear.

"How many acres do you have?" she asked as she dried off with a plush gray towel.

"A little under fifty."

Now that she was back in Vine Grove, she missed the open space and fewer people than California. It was nice to have trees over traffic.

When it was time for bed, Editon showed her to the guest bedroom. When she was in bed, he came in and sat on the side of the bed. He tucked a strand of hair behind her ear and watched her for a long moment before saying, "You have no idea how much I want to break that bond of chivalry

I stupidly set up earlier."

"You don't have to leave." She touched his cheek.

"I said it, and I'm sticking to it. I want to take things slow and not mess this up. I want that second, third, and twenty-fifth date…so,…" Editon let out a sigh before adding, "goodnight." He kissed her again and then left.

Kady listened to the wind against the side of the house and thought about how things had shifted so suddenly. Was she ready to try again? As she drifted off to sleep, she felt Editon's kisses still on her lips.

Chapter Six

Kady thought that she would miss not having a teaching position yet, but she liked her job at the wine shop, and when the time was right it would come. She saw Editon every night for the next week. As the weather dragged on through November, when she was off work, she spent a few hours at his shop laughing and telling him what happened during the day.

This is what a relationship is supposed to be. She'd never had a man who asked how *her* day was or was willing to talk to her if she'd had a bad one. Finn invited her and Editon over for Thanksgiving dinner. Kady was able to swing both meals and not hurt her mother's feeling by having one dinner early and then traveling to Finn's after that.

One afternoon, Editon asked if she could bring Noah with her to his shop after school.

"What does he want to see me for?" Noah asked.

Kady shrugged. "He said that there was something he wanted to talk to you about."

When they arrived at the shop, Noah followed her inside and dropped his backpack on the floor.

Editon was covered in grease as he popped up from behind a motor that he was working on. "Hey! Good to see both of you."

"I brought Noah from school. I didn't want him walking over here on the icy roads," she said.

"Mom...I am old enough to walk home by myself," Noah grumbled.

"I know. It's the other cars on the icy roads I don't trust," Kady stated, as she sat on the corner of Editon's desk. "Why did you want us to come in?"

Editon wiped his hands on an old towel. "I need some help around here, and I was hoping that I could hire Noah after school to help me?"

Noah's eyes narrowed. "Why me?"

"I heard you were good with projects, and I have lots of projects around here." Editon smiled, but Noah didn't return it. "I also need help finishing the lower level of my house."

"I don't know how to do any of that," Noah said.

"Neither did I when I started. You can learn, and I can teach you the things you aren't sure of. Are you interested?" Editon asked and then took a sip of water from a bottle on the desk.

"I don't think so." Noah got up and headed to the door. "Can we go, Mom? I have homework."

Kady looked from Noah to Editon. "Sorry." When Noah walked out the door, she lowered her voice and said, "It's a great opportunity and thanks for thinking of Noah. I'll try and talk to him."

She gave Editon a quick kiss and left.

****

Noah watched his grandfather put the worm on his fishing pole and then drop it into the lake. Their small metal boat rocked in the breeze. It was cold enough that their breath made little clouds in the air as they sat in silence. Even though he was older, Noah had to admit that he still loved fishing with his grandpa.

"Will there still be fish this time of year?" Noah asked as he took the pole from his grandpa.

"Oh, sure." Grandpa still had a hint of a Midwest in his voice.

"I didn't think you usually fished this late in the season."

"Often I don't, but I thought we needed a little man on

man time without the ladies around."

Noah nodded and dipped the end of the pole to jiggle the line.

"I overheard Kady and your grandma talking in the kitchen last night. Kady told her that her new friend Editon offered you a job, and you turned him down."

"Friend? Is that what she calls Editon?" Noah asked and blew out a huff.

"Listen, your mom's been through a lot and from what I've heard, hasn't had too many good men either. Editon has done a lot for this town, and no one I know has a bad thing to say about him."

"I guess I don't know him that well."

"Do you think maybe that's why he made the offer? I think it sounds like a win-win. You two can get to know each other better, and he'll pay you to work." Grandpa dropped his fishing line into the water. "I'm sure you could use a bit of your own money."

"I'm worried that he's going to be another one of the guys that hurt her."

"I don't think he's that kind of guy. I asked around. I'm still Kady's dad and protective." He gave Noah a wry smile. "They told me he's not a love 'em and leave 'em kind of fellow. I see the way Editon looks at Kady when they are together. It's the same way I looked at your grandma...still do. When you have a special someone in your life, someday, you'll understand."

Noah gave him a sideways glance wondering if he should say anything. He took a deep breath and then his words tumbled out, "I really like this girl at school. She's so beautiful, and she's smart. She wants me to join the debate club. I did so I can see her after school."

"I didn't know that."

"I didn't say anything. She's Native American...like Editon. Naira told me about the community center that he's going to build and that all the kids in the area are really excited about it."

His grandpa scratched his chin. "Well, I didn't know that either."

"I think I figured this out on my own. Editon's a pretty nice guy, and maybe I made a mistake by telling him no."

"I think that you should think about it a little more until you give your final answer."

Just then, Noah's pole danced. The line jerked once, twice, and then he started to reel it in. "I've got something!"

"Looks like dinner's on you tonight," his grandpa said using the net to scoop up the fish as it broke the surface of the water.

****

Editon looked up, as the door of his shop opened. He had to admit, he was surprised to see it was Noah.

"Noah? Hey, I didn't expect to see you here."

The boy took his backpack off his arm. "I was walking

back from school and hoped that you would be here."

"What can I do for you?"

"I've been thinking about your offer to work for you...with you. But, I have a few questions."

"Sure." Editon pulled two sodas from the mini fridge and handed one to Noah. They sat on the broken down couch on the side of the shop.

"Do you like my mom?"

Editon tried not to choke on the drink he'd just taken. Noah got right to the point. He paused for a moment before saying, "Yes, I do. I like her a lot."

"I think she likes you too. I know my mom hadn't planned on being a single mom. She always puts me first and not herself. Mom told me that you have this big, huge house and that you kidded that you don't need all of it."

"Yeah..." Noah laughed. "I did tell her that."

"Did my mom tell you what happened, I mean, about our trailer in California?" Noah stared at the can in his hand.

"She told me what happened."

"I didn't do it, but I was responsible. It was because of me that those losers did what they did." Noah bit his lip and wrung his hands. "Mom gave up everything for me, and all I did was burn down our house and most everything we had."

"It wasn't your fault."

"You can tell me that, but I don't believe it. I want to make it up to her. I can't pay back everything, but at least I can do something. If I work after school, every day I can help finish the lower level of your house. If we finish it, will you let my mom and me move in there? You know, like an apartment?"

"Would it be difficult for you?" Editon asked. "You know, with me and your mom dating?"

"I like a girl, too. I understand that you want to be with her as much as you can. It's not weird. I checked you out. I guess you're okay. Grandpa likes you."

"He does?" Editon tried to keep the surprise out of his

voice.

"Yeah, and I know my mom does too, and so does Naira, that's the girl I like. If I work for you, then I can save up and maybe pay you some of the rent."

Editon's heart broke as Noah laid his heart out on the line. He wanted to give him a hug, but guys just didn't do that. "I think that sounds like a great plan."

"I'm just a teenager, and there is only so much I can do. I can accept this, but sitting around and doing nothing is the worst thing I can do."

"I know all about that." Editon smiled. "Noah, what you just said is the start of being a man. Because you love your mom, you are doing something unselfish. *This* is being a man."

Noah brushed his bangs out of his eyes. "When can I start?"

"What about now? I can finish up here and then we can go back to the house to start deciding what building supplies we need for the house." He held out his hand. "Shake on it?"

Noah shook his hand. "One more thing. Can we keep this between you and me until we get it finished? I want it to be a surprise."

Noah kept his word. Every day he was there working hard, except for the debate club days, and then he'd be there a little later. Editon showed Noah how to hang Sheetrock, put in tile and carpet, and complete the finishing work. Noah even asked if he could stay and work while Editon left to meet Kady for dinner.

Kady was right, Noah was a fast learner and a smart kid. Noah was in upper lever math classes, and it made Editon feel good that he could help Noah with his homework.

Noah and Kady began to feel like family. Would they think of him the same way?

Chapter Seven

Kady sang along to the Christmas carols as the downtown came alive with festive lights and holiday decorations. Editon's warm fingers were wrapped around her's. Snow fell lightly from the sky, dusting the sidewalks and trees with fluffy, white flakes.

"I love Christmas!" Kady exclaimed.

"So do I. I like all the holidays from Halloween on. Spending Thanksgiving with Finn and Keaton, everyone felt like family," Editon said and squeezed her hand.

Kady looked around. "This is my first Christmas back in Vine Grove, but I'm surprised that Tegan and the rest of the gang aren't here. I thought they said they were coming."

Editon shrugged. "The holidays are a busy time for everyone. It looks like they are finished lighting the tree.

Would you mind if we stopped by my house on the way to yours? I need to pick up something."

"Sure. I just want to get home before it gets too late. I don't want to leave Noah and Mom and Dad on Christmas Eve."

There was a twinkle in his eyes. "I'm sure they'll be fine. You don't need to worry about them."

"What are you up to? You have been grinning all night." She put a hand on her hip.

"Nothing at all. I told you that I love Christmas." He kissed the tip of her nose as they headed back to his truck.

Editon turned the truck into his driveway. As they drew closer to the house, Kady saw that all the lights were on, and there were a bunch of cars parked in the driveway.

"What is going on?" she asked.

"You'll see soon enough." He turned off the ignition, got out, and then walked around the side to open her door.

"Noah has a surprise for you."

"Noah? Why would Noah be here?"

"Stop with all the questions! If you follow me, all of your questions will be answered."

Instead of going to the front of the house, he walked her to the lower level that led to the basement. Editon opened the door to a booming shout of 'Surprise!'"

She saw her mom and dad, Tegan and all of her new friends from the wine shop, and in the middle of the group, Noah.

Kady walked toward Noah. He grinned from ear to ear. "Welcome home, Mom."

"What? What are you talking about?" she glanced around the room.

Editon came beside her and took her hand. "Noah's been coming here every day after school to help me get the lower level of my house finished. He came up with a plan and asked if the two of you could move in here when it was done. With the money Noah's earned, he's paid the first and last month's rent."

Kady's dad walked to her and put a hand on her arm. "I know this is a surprise, but Noah wanted it this way."

"It needs a little more furniture and Editon said he'd give me a loan to buy a TV and an Xbox." Noah kissed her on the cheek. "I know I didn't cause the fire in California, but this way, I feel that I can help make that up to you. I've seen you cry too often and I wanted to make you smile. The night we came back, I believed what you told me. You were right, things got better."

Kady felt a tear slip from her eye and run down her cheeks. She sniffed and wiped at it.

Noah's eyes grew wide. "Mom, I thought you'd be happy about this."

Editon wiped the tears from Kady's other cheek and smiled at Noah. "She *is* happy, Noah. She's very happy."

Her dad cut her off, "I gave my blessings. It's been

great having the two of you living at our house, but let's face it, there just isn't the room. Noah needs his own room, and I want my couch back at night." He chuckled.

She looked around at the pale yellow walls with the navy blue accents. There was a couch and a few chairs with a pellet stove in the corner for heat, and a small kitchen in the corner.

Tegan stepped closer. "I helped the boys with a few decorating choices. Noah and Editon gave me some hints and working with you, I kind of knew your taste. We wanted to get just a few things to get you and Noah settled and then you can pick the rest."

Kady picked up a carved little wooden bird off the table. "This is from the shop. I loved this."

"I remembered what you said. That was really the first thing we got for the place." Tegan gave her a hug.

"You did all this work in just a few weeks?" Kady asked Editon, still trying to let it all sink in.

"With Noah's help, and then August and a few others came over when they could," Editon said.

"Even my debate club came over. I told them they could have some meetings here after Christmas. I hope that's okay." Noah took the girl next to him by the hand. "Mom, this is Naira."

The dark-eyed girl stepped forward and held out here hand. "It's nice to meet you, Ms. Randall. Noah and I are in debate club together."

Kady shook the girl's hand and then took note, as Naira took Noah's hand again. "I think I have missed a lot in the past month."

"I didn't think we were going to get it done, but it was important to Noah. He wanted it to be a Christmas present," Editon said, and then grinned.

"It's the best Christmas present ever," Kady said. "But, Dad, are you all right with me living under Editon's roof? I know you're old-fashioned, and I don't want to upset you after all that you've done for Noah and me."

"I think it will be all right," her dad said and took her mom's hand.

Editon smiled. "Your dad said that it would be all right if I married you 'pretty soon.' I'm not sure what *that* time frame is, so I didn't want to upset him." Editon reached in his pocket dropped to one knee and opened the box. "I know it's speeding things up. I was going to wait for a few more months, but I just can't. Kady, will you marry me?"

She stared at the ring box and then looked at Noah.

"You deserve to be happy, Mom. Editon's a great guy. If you want to say yes, please do it. Say yes." Noah smiled.

She looked back at Editon and said barely above a whisper, "Yes. Yes, I'll marry you."

He slipped the ring on her finger, stood, and enveloped her in a giant hug. Then he took her face and kissed her. "I love you, Kady."

"I love you, too." She grabbed him and kissed him

again."

All of her friends and family applauded, then came up to them one by one and gave them hugs.

"I jumped the gun saying the house was the best Christmas present ever. Now, I think that you have added to that." She tipped her hand from side to side. It was a gold band with Native American carvings intermixed with colored stone.

Editon rubbed a thumb along the ring. "I wanted to give you a reason to stay in Vine Grove, and I hope that reason can be me."

"The night I left California, I thought I'd hit rock bottom. I guess I had in a way, but you know what that means, there is nowhere to go but up. That night, when we came home to Vine Grove I realized I had everything that was important. I had my mom and dad, and Noah." She gave her son a big hug.

Editon looked down at her. "Did you notice that you

just referred to Vine Grove as home? I guess that we were always waiting for you to come home and for me to have a second chance."

She grinned at him. "I don't think you ever got the first chance, so technically, this is your first chance."

"When it comes to you, every chance is the first chance. I can't tell you that it's going to be easy in the next year. I'll have a lot on my plate with building the new community center. You may not see much of me for a while."

"I know where to find you," Kady said and then added, "Why don't we have the wedding reception there when it's finished?"

Editon frowned. "I don't know how long it's going to take to build."

"I can wait. I've waited this long to find love, I can wait on the community center."

He laughed. "Only if you let me make it the first event

booked there."

"It's a deal," she said. "Want to shake on it? My dad taught me to always shake on a deal."

"How about a kiss instead?" He grabbed her and kissed her until they were both out of breath. When he stepped back, he said, "I knew that Christmas was always my favorite holiday."

She kissed him. "I looked for so long, and I found that what I really wanted was a home for Christmas. The people of Vine Grove and you gave me that." -

Christmas was great, but Kady was looking forward to all the others holidays throughout the year, as long as she could spend them with Editon.

Look for the other stories in

The Christmas Love List Series

Surprise! You're a Christmas Bride
Natalie-Nicole Bates
Story 1

New to town, all that bridal consultant Maisey Gates wants is to meet a few new friends at Christmas time. When they introduce her to The Love List as a way to find that special Christmas date, Maisey wants no parts of it, but she doesn't want to disappoint her new friends.

Love finds Maisey before she even has a chance to look at her Love List match.
Sean Marshall is ready to resume his life after tragically losing his wife. Meeting Maisey is a breath of fresh air, and he immediately senses Maisey could become a

permanent part of his life. But Sean has a lot of baggage, some of it potential deal-breakers for his new relationship with Maisey.

What Sean doesn't know is Maisey has a secret of her own.

With Christmas fast approaching, will Maisey and Sean find their Merry Christmas together, or will it be another holiday spent alone?

Christmas Kisses & Wishes
Sharon Kleve
Story 2

After her husband divorced her, Finn Dubose packed up her dog Scorch, gathered what was left of her dignity and set out on a twelve month adventure to find happiness.

After nine months of traveling from Florida, to Colorado, and then to Maine, all Finn wants is to go back to Charleston, South Carolina and spend the holidays with her grandmother. But reluctantly, Finn promises Gran she'll spend the last three months of the year in Seattle, Washington.

The spectacular vineyards in Eastern Washington entice Finn to drive from Seattle to the small town of Vine Grove. What she finds is a place full of kind, generous people, including, Keaton Vanhorn, a single, attractive, veterinarian. Even better, he loves animals as much as Finn.

Sometimes, a bottle of wine and The Love List is all you need to find love. Stop by the small town of Vine Grove and maybe you'll be lucky in love too

Christmas Country Wishes
Angela Ford
Story 4

Dakota Timmons, a registered nurse, leaves the bustling city life for small town comfort in Washington's wine country. As a child she wished for a white Christmas. As an adult, her wish remains the same along with a new one. Vine Grove is exactly what she needs. She only hopes she's what the doctor ordered. Or that he at least accepts her shocking news.

Avoiding an accident by seconds on her way into town introduces Dakota to Tristan Hart. Instant attraction makes them both think about love for the first time in their demanding careers. He calls her Miss Country Girl and in her mind she calls him Mr. Stetson. Under his Stetson, this man has the most piercing eyes, a striking blue-green combination. They remind her of the Pacific tropical seas.

She's absorbed in thought to meet the man she'd changed her zip code for, but she's reminded of Tristan when she joins her new friends for a wine and chat night. A basket is placed on her lap. She's to pick a name from it and then ask him out. A wild idea but she agrees to play a game called The Love List. To her surprise, she picks Tristan Hart. Now the man she'd changed her zip code for may not be the only man on her mind.

Love Uncorked
Love Found Me
Blind Tasting
Building up to Love

About the Author
Jennifer Conner

Jennifer Conner is a best-selling Northwest author who has seventy short stories, books, and audiobooks. She writes in Christmas Romance, Contemporary Romance, Paranormal Romance, Historical Romance, and Erotica.

She has hit Amazon's top fifty authors ranking and her books have been #1 in sales.

Her novel Shot in the Dark was a finalist in the Emerald City Opener, Cleveland, and Toronto RWA contests. Jennifer is an Associate Publisher for the indie e-book publisher, Books to Go Now who resides in the Seattle area. They pride themselves in helping new authors get their foot in the door with well-edited manuscripts, professional covers, and platforms uploads.

She lives in a hundred year old house that she grew up in. Her semi-small town holds an interesting mix of resident hillbillies, yuppies and Navy Seals. And of course Seattle, only a few miles away, is the birthplace of Starbucks so coffee is always on the check list. She blows glass beads with a blow torch, (which relieves a lot of stress and people don't bother you) and is a huge fan of musicals.

She loves to hear from her readers. Please email her at jenniferconnerwriter@gmail.com

For Updates about new releases as well as exclusive promotions, visit Jennifer's website and sign up for the VIP mailing list. http://www.jenniferconnerbooks.com/

Look for Jennifer Conner's Other Titles
BOOKS AVAILABLE IN EBOOK, PAPERBACK, AUDIOBOOK, and FOREIGN LANGUAGE

Novels
Shot in the Dark
Kilt by Love
Coming Soon - Sleep Fall

Kindle World
Carly Phillips Dare World
London on a Dare
Bella Andre Four Weddings and a Fiasco World
The Wedding Bridesmaid

Sweet Romances
Love on the Airwaves
Love Uncorked
Christmas Dog Tails
Christmas at Central Bark
Christmas Gift that Keeps Wagging
Dog Tags for Christmas
Love Comes for Valentine's Day
Love Comes for Saint Patrick's Day
Love Comes for the 4th of July
Love Comes for Halloween
I Hear Angels
Brewing up Some Love
Valentine Surprise
Cupcakes and Cupids
Christmas Chaos
The Christmas Horse
All I Want for Christmas is You
All I Want for Christmas is You

Sexy Romances
Bad Boy's Second Chance
Cinderella Had it Easy
Love Potion Number 10
Ten Minutes for Christmas
In Love With Santa
The Music of Christmas
Make Me Burn
Winner Takes All
Valentine Encounter
New Year Resolution
Christmas with Carol
Auld Lang Sigh
Rush of Love
Fields of Gold
The Music of Christmas

Historical
The Duke and the Lost Night
The Wounded Nobleman
The Reluctant Heir
Redemption for a Rogue

Time Travel
I'll be Seeing You Through Time
Walk with me Through Time

Anthologies
Handmade for Christmas Series
The Love List Series
The Pancake Club Collection
A Christmas Kiss is on the List Anthology
Love in Time for Christmas Anthology

A Home for Christmas

Christmas Romance (Best of Christmas Romances 2013) Anthology
Love Under the Christmas Tree Anthology
The Mobile Mistletoe Boxed Set
The Regimental Heroes Boxed Set
Yours for Christmas Anthology
Valentine's Say I Love You

You can find more stories such as this at www.bookstogonow.com

If you enjoy this Books to Go Now story please leave a review for the author on Amazon, Goodreads or the site which you purchased the ebook. Thanks!

We pride ourselves with representing great stories at low prices. We want to take you into the digital age offering a market that will allow you to grow along with us in our journey through the new frontier of digital publishing.
Some of our favorite award-winning authors have now joined us. We welcome readers and writers into our community.

We want to make sure that as a reader you are supplied with never-ending great stories. As a company, Books to Go Now, wants its readers and writers supplied with positive experience and encouragement so they will return again and again.

We want to hear from you. Our readers and writers are the cornerstone of our company. If there is something you would like to say or a genre that you would like to see, please email us at inquiry@bookstogonow.com